TALES OF BUTTERCUP GROVE

A Windy Spring Day

By WENDY DUNHAM
ILLUSTRATED BY MICHAL SPARKS

HARVEST HOUSE PUBLISHERS
EUGENE, OREGON

The Scripture quotation on page 64 is from the *Holy Bible*, New Living Translation, copyright © 1996, 2004, 2007, 2013 by Tyndale House Foundation. Used by permission of Tyndale House Publishers, Inc., Carol Stream, Illinois 60188. All rights reserved.

Cover design by Mary Eakin

Interior design by Janelle Coury

Published in association with William K. Jensen Literary Agency, 119 Bampton Court, Eugene, Oregon 97404.

HARVEST KIDS is a registered trademark of The Hawkins Children's LLC. Harvest House Publishers, Inc., is the exclusive licensee of the federally registered trademark HARVEST KIDS.

A WINDY SPRING DAY

Copyright © 2018 by Wendy Dunham
Artwork © 2018 by Michal Sparks

Published by Harvest House Publishers
Eugene, Oregon 97402
www.harvesthousepublishers.com

ISBN 978-0-7369-7200-0 (hardcover)
ISBN 978-0-7369-7201-7 (eBook)

Library of Congress Cataloging-in-Publication Data
Names: Dunham, Wendy, author. | Sparks, Michal, illustrator.
Title: A windy spring day / Wendy Dunham ; illustrations by Michal Sparks.
Description: Eugene, Oregon : Harvest House Publishers, 2018. | Summary: Skunk is afraid when the wind is strong enough to shake his house, but his friend, Raccoon, arrives with a surprise, that makes Skunk feel much better.
Identifiers: LCCN 2017016832 (print) | LCCN 2017035615 (ebook) | ISBN 9780736972017 (ebook) | ISBN 9780736972000 (hardcover)
Subjects: | CYAC: Kites—Fiction. | Fear—Fiction. | Friendship—Fiction. | Animals—Fiction. | Spring—Fiction.
Classification: LCC PZ7.1.D86 (ebook) | LCC PZ7.1.D86 Win 2018 (print) | DDC [E]—dc23
LC record available at https://lccn.loc.gov/2017016832

Printed in China

18 19 20 21 22 23 24 25 26 / RDS-JC / 10 9 8 7 6 5 4 3 2

1

Skunk Needs a Friend

It was a windy day and Skunk was home alone. He was afraid. Skunk curled up in the corner of his couch. "It is so windy that my house is shaking," he cried.

Skunk pulled a blanket over his head.
"I know," he said, "I will call Raccoon.
Then I will not be afraid."

Skunk ran to his phone.
"Hello, Raccoon. Is it windy at your
house?"

"Yes," said Raccoon. "It is very windy."

Skunk's house shook again.

"Is it so windy that your house is shaking?" he asked.

"Yes," said Raccoon. "My house is shaking."

Skunk peeked out from under his blanket.

"Is it so windy that you are afraid?"

"It is windy," said Raccoon.
"But I am not afraid."

"Then why am I afraid?" asked Skunk.

"Because you are silly," said Raccoon.
"But do not worry. I will come to
your house."

Skunk was surprised.

"You will come to my house?" he said.

"How did you know what I needed?"

Raccoon smiled. "Skunk, I have known
you for a long time. I know you are afraid
of the wind. You always need a friend
when it is windy."

"You are a good friend," said Skunk.

"I will be there soon," said Raccoon.
"And I will bring a surprise."

2

Raccoon's Surprise

Raccoon got his backpack. He put many things inside. He put in two long sticks. He put in some newspaper. He put in tape. He put in one pair of scissors.
He put in a big ball of string.
He put in one long piece of ribbon.

Raccoon put his backpack on. Then he walked along the path through Buttercup Grove. The wind pushed him back and forth. But Raccoon was not afraid.

Finally he reached Skunk's house.
Raccoon knocked on the door.

Skunk was still on his couch.
"Come in," Skunk yelled to Raccoon.

When Raccoon touched the door, the wind
blew it open. "Are you still afraid?" asked
Raccoon.

Skunk jumped off his couch and ran to Raccoon. "You are here. Now I am not afraid."

Raccoon took his backpack off. "I will show you the surprise." Raccoon took everything out and set it on the floor.

Skunk looked at the sticks.
He looked at the newspaper.
He looked at the tape.
He looked at the scissors.
He looked at the string.
He looked at the ribbon.

"Do you know what we can make?"
asked Raccoon.

"I do not know," said Skunk.

"We can make a kite!" said Raccoon.

"That is a nice surprise," said Skunk.
"But there is one problem.
I do not know how to make a kite."

"Do not worry," said Raccoon.
"I will teach you."

3

Making the Kite

Raccoon formed a cross with the sticks.
He tied them together in the middle.
"The sticks will make our kite strong,"
he said.

Then Raccoon tied string from each end of the sticks to the others. The string made a shape. It did not look like a circle. It did not look like a square. It did not look like a triangle.

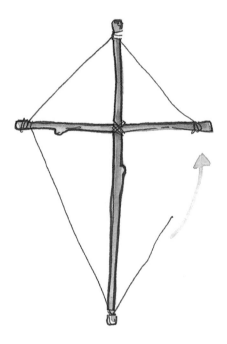

"It looks like a diamond," said Skunk.

"You are right," said Raccoon.
"Our kite is a diamond shape."

Raccoon set the diamond on the newspaper.

He cut around all four sides.

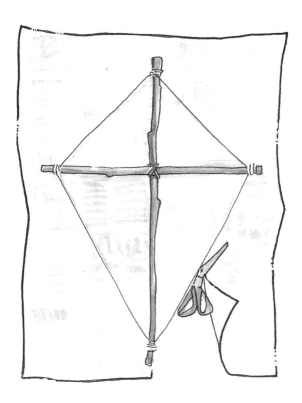

Raccoon gave the tape to Skunk.

"Rip small pieces of tape," said Raccoon. "Then give them to me one at a time."

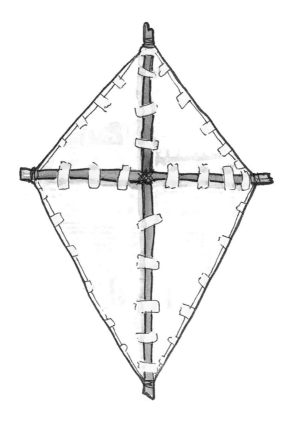

Skunk gave Raccoon small pieces of tape. Raccoon taped the newspaper to the diamond shape.

"Now we will make a tail for our kite,"
said Raccoon.

"A tail?" said Skunk. "That is silly.
I have a tail. And you have a tail.
But why does our kite need a tail?"

"A tail will help our kite fly," said Raccoon.

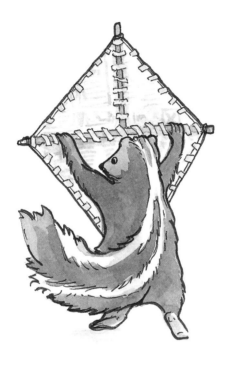

"But our tails do not help us fly,"
said Skunk.

"We are not a kite," said Raccoon.
"A kite is different."

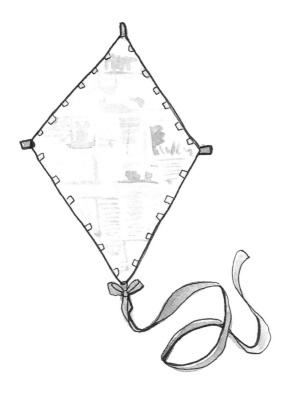

Raccoon took the long piece of ribbon.
He tied it to the bottom of the kite.

"There," he said, "now our kite has a tail."

Next, Raccoon took the ball of string.
He tied the end to the middle of the kite.

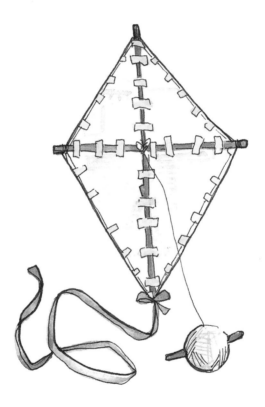

"Our kite is ready to fly," said Raccoon.

"But we are not ready," said Skunk.

"What do we need?" asked Raccoon.

"We need our friends," said Skunk.
"They will want to see the kite fly too."

"You are right," said Raccoon.

Skunk ran to his phone. First he called Mouse. Then he called Rabbit, Mole, Beaver, and Fox. "Hurry and come to my house," he said. "Raccoon and I have a surprise for you."

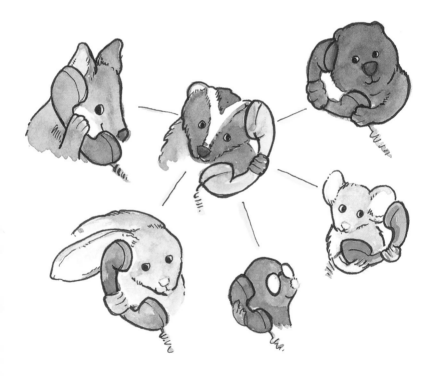

4

Sharing the Surprise

Mouse, Rabbit, Mole, Beaver, and Fox
hurried through Buttercup Grove
to Skunk's house.

"We are here!" they shouted.
"We cannot wait to see the surprise!"

Raccoon held the kite
so everyone could see.

"That is a wonderful kite," said Mouse.

"It is a good thing it is windy," said Beaver.

"Will it fly?" asked Rabbit.

"We will find out," said Raccoon.

Raccoon gave the kite to Skunk. But
Raccoon held the ball of string.

"When I say 'go,'" said Raccoon, "run fast.
Then give the kite to the wind."

"How can I give the kite to the wind?" asked Skunk. "The wind does not have hands to take it."

"The wind will take it," said Raccoon. "You will see."

Raccoon yelled so everyone could hear.
"Get ready! Get set! Go!"

Skunk held the kite up high.
He ran across the yard.
He ran down the hill.
He ran as fast as he could.

All of a sudden the wind took the kite.
It flew high into the air. Higher and higher
it went. It waved back and forth across
the sky. Its tail followed close behind.

Everyone took turns flying the kite.

"This is a very happy day," said Raccoon.

"And a very windy day," said Mouse.

Skunk smiled as the wind blew his furry tail. "And I am not afraid!"

"When I am afraid,
I will put my trust in you."

Psalm 56:3